TICKLED PINK

How Friendship Washes the World with Color

By Andrée Poulin

Illustrated by Lucile Danis Drouot

pajamapress

Zac the zebra and Poncho the panda are like two peas in a pod.
"Can I play with you?" asks Filippo.
"No!"

Zac tries to think of an excuse. "You're too pink," he says.
"Pink gives me a headache," says Poncho.
The little flamingo flushes.

Filippo asks his mother,
"Does pink give people headaches?"

"Not at all!" cries Filippo's mother. "Pink is the color of kindness."
"And of happiness," adds his father.

Zac and Poncho are still having fun.

"Pink is the color of happiness," Filippo tells them.

Zac and Poncho pretend not to hear.

"I can be the goalie if you want," Filippo offers.
Poncho rolls his eyes. "We don't want you to play."
"Pink doesn't mix with black and white," says Zac.

Filippo asks his grandma, "Can't pink mix with black and white?"
"Of course it can!" says his grandma. "When the sun sets, it
paints the sky pink. When the pink mixes with all the other
colors, it's beautiful! And delightful! And wonderful!"

With the tip of her paintbrush, Grandma paints a pretty black dot
on her grandson's beak. Then a dainty white dot. Filippo laughs.
It gives him an idea.

"Can I play with you now?" asks Filippo.
"You look ridiculous," says Zac.

"What a mess," adds Poncho.

An hour later, Filippo is back. "Can I play with you now?"
Zac shakes his head. "You're still too pink. And pink is for
babies and princesses."

"I don't like babies. They cry too much," says Poncho.
"And princesses are too fussy."

Filippo's big sister Flavia lands in a flurry of feathers.
"Why are you crying?"
"I don't want to be pink," sobs Filippo.
"Pink is for crybabies and silly princesses."
"Where on earth did you get that idea?" Flavia demands.
"Pink is for everyone. Everything I love is pink: cotton candy, strawberry ice cream—even my little brother."

Filippo races over to Zac and Poncho and yells,
"Pink is for everyone!"

Zac and Poncho stick their tongues out
and go back to their game.

All day, Ludo the lemur has been too shy to step in. But now he comes up to Filippo and whispers, "If pink didn't exist, there would be no shrimp. No salmon. No bubble gum."

Filippo raises his head. More loudly, Ludo goes on. "Without pink, we wouldn't have cherry blossoms or begonias. No peonies or petunias. And no roses!"

Ludo smiles at Filippo. "I'm black and white, but I'd love to play with you." His voice trembling, Filippo asks, "You mean it?"

"I mean it," says Ludo. "And I have a good idea for adding some more pink to the world. Are you with me?"

The zebra and the panda are not amused...

...but lots of other animals
are tickled pink to go pink.

And so is Filippo.

First published in Canada and the United States in 2020

Text copyright © 2019 Andrée Poulin
Illustration copyright © 2019 Lucile Danis Drouot
This edition copyright © 2020 Pajama Press Inc.
Original French edition copyright © 2019 Éditions Héritage inc. / Dominique et compagnie, Quebec, Canada J4R 1P8

10 9 8 7 6 5 4 3 2 1

 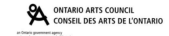

The publisher gratefully acknowledges the support of the Canada Council for the Arts and the Ontario Arts Council for its publishing program. We acknowledge the financial support of the Government of Canada through the Canada Book Fund (CBF) for our publishing activities.

Library and Archives Canada Cataloguing in Publication

Title: Tickled pink / by Andrée Poulin ; illustrated by Lucile Danis Drouot.
Other titles: Ils ne veulent pas jouer avec moi!!! English
Names: Poulin, Andrée, author. | Danis Drouot, Lucile, 1980- illustrator.
Description: Translation of: Ils ne veulent pas jouer avec moi!!!
Identifiers: Canadiana 20190165901 | ISBN 9781772781045 (hardcover)
Classification: LCC PS8581.O837 I4713 2020 | DDC jC843/.54—dc23

Publisher Cataloging-in-Publication Data (U.S.)

Names: Poulin, Andrée, author. | Danis Drouot, Lucile, 1980- , illustrator.
Title: Tickled Pink / by Andrée Poulin, illustrated by Lucile Danis Drouot.
Description: Toronto, Ontario Canada : Pajama Press, 2019. | Originally published in French by Dominique et Companie, 2019 as: Ils Ne Veulent Pas Jouer Avec Moi!!! | Summary: "A young flamingo named Filippo becomes self-conscious when other animals refuse to play with him because he is pink. He struggles to be accepted and to accept himself. Finally, with encouragement from family members and a kind-hearted lemur, Filippo learns to love himself for who he is"— Provided by publisher.
Identifiers: ISBN 978-1-77278-104-5 (hardback)
Subjects: LCSH: Bullying – Juvenile fiction. | Rejection (Psychology) -- Juvenile fiction. | Flamingos – Juvenile fiction. | BISAC: JUVENILE FICTION / Social Themes / Self-Esteem & Self-Reliance. | JUVENILE FICTION / Social Themes / Emotions & Feelings.
Classification: LCC PZ7.P685Ti |DDC [E] – dc23

Original art created with traditional and digital media.

Manufactured by Qualibre Inc./Printplus
Printed in China

Pajama Press Inc.
181 Carlaw Ave. Suite 251 Toronto, Ontario Canada, M4M 2S1

Distributed in Canada by UTP Distribution
5201 Dufferin Street Toronto, Ontario Canada, M3H 5T8

Distributed in the U.S. by Ingram Publisher Services
1 Ingram Blvd. La Vergne, TN 37086, USA

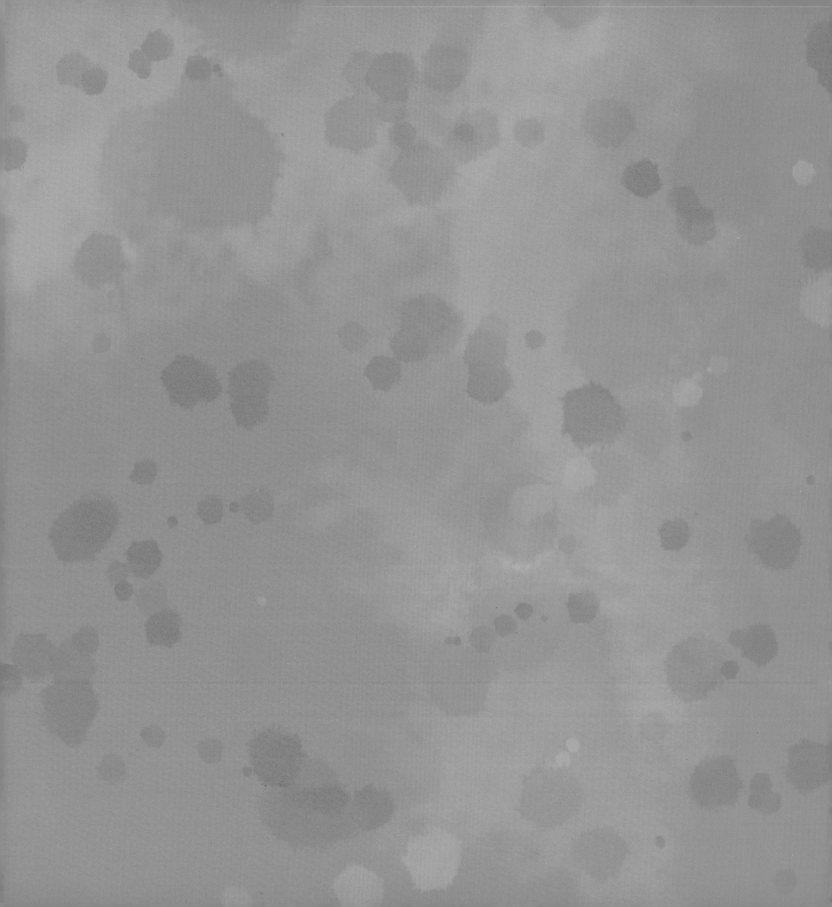